Dangerous Playthings

a dark little tale
of love among the ruins

by
Della Van Hise
author of the most controversial
Star Trek **novel ever published**

For Wendy...

Dangerous Playthings

It would be night soon.

The thought caused Merkinder an ironic moment. It was always night now. Close enough anyway. No reason to draw the blinds or board up the windows to parcel out the dawn. It was a relief, though he did occasionally miss the whole drama of sunrise, sunset, night takes day, day rapes night, when the world had tick-tocked along some rickety track of Time and the humans went about their business as if none of it would ever change.

But it did change. As Merkinder had known it would. He'd seen it before. He would see it again. That was his nature. To be the observer, the incarnate gnosis of the silence at the edge of all things. There was a name for his kind, but that, too, changed with the eons.

Darkling.

Immortal.

Vampyrr.

Demon.

Angel. Sprite.

Faerie lord.

Elemental.

He'd lost track of it all centuries ago. Words may be pregnant with poetry, but entirely still-born in the end. For now, he was simply Merkinder.

He looked out the cracked windows and saw only the scent of salt, felt only the taste of smoke from the campfires up in the forested hills, where the humans huddled together and sang desperate prayers to a world that had died long, long before they were born. Eerie ballads of the damned, sung to the malignant gods who had destroyed them, minor-keyed melodies plucked out on hollow gourds strung with sinew harvested from the dead.

If not so ironic, it might have been comical.

Merkinder's home was once a house, back in the days before The Fall. Mostly buried by an avalanche of sand and debris, now it more closely resembled a foreboding cave sunk deep into the crags of the cliffside which was once an affluent neighborhood at the lip of the western sea. With the coming of ever-autumn, and in absolute defiance of scientific prediction, a thick growth of foliage had covered most of the earth – including the roof and exterior walls and windows, leaving only a single entrance at what had been the front of the elegant home. Not *his* home. Merkinder was vagabond and gypsy moth. Hermit crab and squatter. The house suited him after The Fall and as there were no politicians or governments to tell him otherwise, he took it as his own.

The double-oak doors and half of what had once been a massive window overlooking the rocky shoreline were the only surface even remotely visible to prying eyes, but no eyes came to pry other than Willow LeBlanc, for gone were the days when humans would come to the beach to lounge in the sun or surf the waves with their colorful toys filled with air and hope and dreams that had turned to nightmares when the comet known as Denizen struck the earth.

The sun was all but gone, as were the waves. Now the sea was still, a grim glass eye, molten grey jello shivering in its lifeless bed, waiting for what would surely be the welcome breath of a black hole to suck the entire world into final, merciful death.

All realities were self-created at the sub-atomic level, where thought and energy flirted and danced and fucked their way into manifestation. Maybe nobody had outright wished for Denizen, but it was no coincidence that the comet came out of the Nothing at a time when civilization had run its course. Just the janitor of space and time, sweeping up the aftermath of humanity, leaving little in its wake, the ultimate jack-off do-over.

Nowadays, there were no days per se, only unbending dusk, barely enough light to keep the plants alive – oddly adapting and tangling together, vines of red, purple and gold growing like fiery leaves from cinder-trees, cactus and lilies and pumpkins propagating more rapidly than mutated wildflowers, until all the world resembled some ghastly witch-garden gone amuck, where the sun shone for maybe four hours out of twenty-four, just a dim red dime, fleeting orb always low on the horizon, wallowing from one end of the north to the other, miscreant piñata.

Immortality meant having time on one's hands, and so Merkinder had wandered the earth for more than a hundred years since The Fall, and near as he could determine, it was the same everywhere. No miraculous pockets of surviving civilization. No sanctuary with internet hotspots and pompous turds in business suits chasing tail. This was the world now – a world that no longer remembered computers or night clubs or high-rise corporations.

It both quickened and troubled Merkinder to see Willow LeBlanc silhouetted against the melancholy blush of sky, black watercolor on maroon canvas, crescent moon just above, and tipped playfully in such a manner that it seemed to protrude from her forehead like a single golden horn.

"You'll break my heart," he heard himself say, though he couldn't be sure if he spoke aloud or if the voice came from Madness, who was always at his side, even when not visible to the naked eye.

Willow was too old for this. What was she now? 13? 14? When time had lost all meaning, so did age, and yet he could smell the sweet syrup of womanhood in her veins that hadn't been there just a few months before. Children were supposed to grow up, leave *his* world behind, and eventually grow old and die. What was it about her that seemed determined to defy the paradigm? He had taught her all the could from the old books salvaged from devastated libraries and his own private collection. Why did she still come?

He took a quick, sharp breath – the first in at least a century.

After The Fall, when the world trembled in the arms of chaos and the aftermath of Denizen, Merkinder had raised dozens of mortal children. Odd, he thought, that humans would bring their offspring and leave them on the beach like feral pups savagely and prematurely torn from their mother's teat.

He had heard the rumors, of course. There was a beast who lived somewhere along the shore, and if one sacrificed a child to the bloodthirsty creature, it might make the sun rise again and the waters return to the rivers and the lights come back on in the colossal villages which had once been called cities. It had taken him some time to realize that *he* was the monster to whom the legends referred; he was the bleak rumor wrapped in whispers and offered the whelps of humans who were no longer very much human at all. Most of the children wandered off into the forests, where they became food for the packs of wild dogs. Others pined for their parents and eventually died of starvation – not from lack of food, but lack of affection, nurturing, human contact. A species that lost the instinct to nourish its young doomed itself to extinction. And yet...

A few of the children... a very select few... Merkinder took to himself to raise, thinking of them as deformed kittens or foundlings or changelings or anything other than the dirty, malnourished, abandoned misfits they were in reality. Maybe he would have taken them all if he'd had the ability, but finding food for five at a time was hard enough. Finding enough for thirty would have been impossible, or at the very least an inconvenience which Merkinder did not care to take upon himself. He was not a nice man. He was not a man at all. Hadn't been a man for a thousand years and some before The Fall.

The cracks in Merkinder's window fractured Willow's silhouette, warping and bending it like a funhouse mirror. Just as he had warped and bent her when he had plucked her from the savage shore along with four others. What had it been? 10 years ago now?

The others had all gone.

Earth.

Air.

Fire.

Water.

That was how he thought of his students, how he named them. Earth and Water were always girl-children. Earth he schooled in the arts of building and growth, while Water was the flow of knowledge who might go back to the humans as the new teacher. Fire and Air were the male children – Fire being the warrior and the hunter and the guardian of mathematics, Air the custodian of the arts – music-maker and mischief-maker, poet and priest of words.

And then there was the matter of Spirit, whose gender was determined by Fate with each new tribe – for he thought of them as his tribe while they were under his care, living under his earthen roof, tending the garden, practicing dance and the fighting arts, and polishing their knowledge until, eventually, the ravages of puberty called them back to the wild, and, one by one, they left his home, never to return.

It was no coincidence that Willow had been his Spirit – pointed out to him by fate. Most of the children, upon being dragged to the shore and left by their parents to die, wept or wailed or screamed until they lost the energy to protest, or created their own end by calling down upon themselves the coyotes and the other predators who were never far away in the ever-dusk, a quick bolt from the edge of the forest to the edge of the sea. The shore was littered with rags and bones, child-ghosts, undefined wraiths who never had the chance to grow up, never the opportunity to earn a face. The blind ones. The ones who howled like banshees now-and-evermore in the night that never ended. At times, Merkinder believed it would drive him even madder than he already was.

But Willow wasn't like the others. She didn't cry. She didn't scream. She wasn't afraid.

Instead, she sang. Not in a particularly beautiful voice, but with an undeniable connection to... *something*.

That *something*, Merkinder knew, was Spirit. And so she had completed his tribe – the fifth element of creation, the one who must carry the blessings and the burdens of metaphysical knowledge: the myths and the legends, the very soul of Rebirth and the bloody scythe of Death – for Spirit was the spark at the heart of all Creation. Without Spirit, the other elements might lay dormant for eternity.

Eternity...

The word rolled over in his mind, faithful companion and savage trickster. The yin and yang of his tumultuous essence.

He remembered the old world vaguely, though he had no idea how long it had been. Immortals told time by the rise and fall of mountains, the course of rivers, the path of comets. And, of course, Time had treated him strangely even before the coming of Denizen – when he would prowl the transient night and drink from the veins of the dark ones, the naughty ones who would otherwise prey on their own kind. It was his job, he had reckoned, the thing Nature had created him to do: exterminator of the wicked, prince of predators, king of the immortals... though he had no real idea why or even how he had become the thing he was back then, the thing he was still now, so many ochre centuries later. His maker had taught him nothing, and at times he wondered if *that* was why he had taken it upon himself to teach the sacrificial lambs – not out of any great sense of nobility, but because they deserved better than he himself had received.

"Don't go getting maudlin again," Madness cautioned with a nasty edge to his voice that might have been the gales screaming through the crags and crannies of the cave house.

"Last time you brought Pompeii down on a bunch of primitives. Tsk tsk tsk."

Merkinder didn't bother pointing out that he hadn't been born yet when Pompeii fell. No point arguing with Madness. So he held his silence, reverenced it.

He watched the girl-thing for a long time, the way November plucked at her tattered dress, tossing her hair around like a luminous halo spun of black widow silk and ragged lace. The wind could have broken her. Instead it flirted with her, as if to suggest that she was one of the rare few who belonged here in this savage new world.

She was her name. Thin. Pale. Yet strong. And she had always been November's child, even though it could have been March or August or the Season of Ash. The world's clocks were all broken, and so Merkinder decided it was the month of Always-November. No agreements sought or required.

Aware that Willow was aware of him, he debated with Madness as to what course of action might be best. He had not spoken with her in months - *his* choice, not hers. She came every day. He came *out* only when it suited him. And it had not suited him lately, for he knew his earlier statement to be true. She would break his heart.

"Leave her for the dogs," Madness suggested without so much as a flinch. "That's her fate anyway, isn't it? Death and worms? The time-honored cycle of life in the mortal world?" Madness reached out with a hand made of cold wind, picking at the roots that had tunneled their way in through the cracks in the once-noble roof. A bit of moist soil dropped onto Merkinder's shoulder.

For a moment, he caught himself looking around the room which had once known human life and merriment and the caress of black cocktail dresses, expensive tuxedoes, the clink of crystal, the scent of wine. Now, the only light came from a handmade candle glowing softly in the earth-covered ruins which would never see sunlight again.

Merkinder brushed the dirt away from the lapel of the suit he had salvaged from the remnants of his former life, from a time when he had dressed up like a man and played the role of the handsome young rogue in the shadows of dive bars and magnificent cathedrals – camouflaged by Nature and Georgio Armani in such a way as to insure that he would never go hungry.

"You've still got your good looks," Madness told him grudgingly. "We could go hunting tonight. Would it really be so terrible? How long has it been? Yes, I think that sounds like a plan, old boy! Shall we?"

"No, we shall *not*," Merkinder said, and this time he was quite certain he spoke aloud, for the sound of his voice reverberated eerily off the walls and windows. His own private tomb, earthen sanctuary, grave of the ancients, Plato's cave. The scent of freshly turned earth and chrysanthemums and the leather upholstery of black limousines filled with mourners. Madness wasn't wrong. It was the cycle of Life, even if not *his* life.

He pushed thoughts of Death aside. Death had eaten his fill of the world. Merkinder's old friend had become his new enemy.

Madness scrutinized him as one might a rebellious gnat. "Oh, come now!" it scolded. "*You*? At war with Death? You've killed more humans than Denizen over the centuries. Don't tell me you've taken up the old rugged cross and decided to become God's little angel. I'm not sure I could stomach that. Might throw up a little in my mouth."

Ignoring his eternal tormentor, Merkinder walked abruptly out into the world without bothering to open the door. A talent bequeathed to him by whatever manner of monster had stolen his humanity all those millennium ago. He could turn to smoke or take the form of coyote or spread himself as fog over the sea just to lie down with her like a lover. But for now, he was content to appear as the man he had been when he was human. A slender shade with dark amber eyes that had seen too much of life, too much of death, too much of Time.

Willow looked up when he appeared on the beach, her pensive expression turning to a playful smile that was far too grown-up, no longer innocent.

"There you are," she said, her voice neither that of a child nor a woman. Somewhere in between. Somewhere in that danger zone. "I was starting to think you'd run away to the far side of the world, like you're always threatening to do."

She moved toward him the way an autumn breeze might move. Confident. Warm but tinged with something potentially foreboding, a smile more ominous than an open grave.

Their relationship had always been one of teacher and student, nothing more. And yet, of all the children he had ever taught, only this one returned now. Merkinder liked to think some of the knowledge he gave them might speed up the process of rebuilding, but the fact was that he didn't know. It was simply what he did. Another task Nature had given him. And never once did he expect any of them to form attachments, for the world was a harsh stage set only for survival of the fittest – too cruel and too cold to allow for affection. Love would have to wait for the Renaissance... and *that*, he knew, might never come again.

Willow came up next to him, so close he could feel the warmth of her, could smell the golden apples and fat pumpkins she had been harvesting from his garden. She was welcome, of course. It wasn't as if Merkinder were a vegetarian, wasn't as if he ate much of anything or any*one* these days. And yet... Willow scared him more than he wanted to be scared. Little Lolita.

"Well?" she prompted. "Aren't you going to tell me what you've been doing that's kept you so busy you couldn't even come out and say hello?"

He felt that stirring – the one in the center of his chest that always spelled trouble. The stirring of a heart that had been broken too many times and finally sealed shut in impenetrable grief where it was no longer vulnerable.

"You shouldn't come here anymore," he told her, surprising even himself with the abruptness in his tone. "Go back to your own people."

She looked at him with wide brown eyes and quirked a smile made of demon feathers and sweet, sweet elderberry wine harvested from faerie groves up in the phantom forest.

"I have no people," she said matter-of-factly. "You gave me the Sight, the Knowing. Why would I want to go back to a bunch of man-boys and end up with babies crawling out of my belly? Where's the fun in that?"

Merkinder tried to remain detached, though she wasn't making it easy for him. She never had. "Come," he said, gesturing toward the endless length of shoreline stretching out toward the south. "Walk with me, girl."

She fell in at his side as if she had always been there – shadow incarnate, reflection manifested. He didn't like the thought. So he focused instead on the taste of copper, the length of a witch's fang, things that made no sense.

Only as he walked did he realize how long it had been since he'd come out of his sanctuary. To his surprise, he heard a sea bird piping somewhere up amongst the trees that had crept closer to shore over the centuries. A bit of wave licked at the cinder-sand, more movement than he'd seen in the water in a long time. Up ahead, far in the distance, a couple of feral cats yowled and fought over a female in heat. To the east, mountains covered in permafrost screamed in voices of the murdered dead.

"I hear them, too," Willow said, kicking her bare feet through the coarse and dirty sand until a pack of dust-devils followed on her heels like curious pets.

Merkinder frowned, looking at the girl-thing more closely. "What do you hear?"

"The lamentations of the ancestors," Willow said casually. "Those who were here before the here got squashed by the falling moon."

"Comet," Merkinder corrected. "Denizen was a comet."

Willow shrugged her small shoulders. "Comet, moon... does it matter? We're all ghosts now, caught in the web of our own creation and destruction." She paused, stopped walking, and looked up at Merkinder. "Well, all except you. Death lost your address."

Something in her tone raised the hairs on the back of Merkinder's neck.

"You're not a ghost, Willow," he told her, keenly aware of that fact as the brisk wind brought him a scent of her blood, the living breath of her. It troubled him to realize he wanted her. Troubled him more to know he had since the first moment he saw her. She was Life incarnate.

She shot him a look that spoke volumes. "No... not a ghost... not yet," she mused. "But soon. Always too soon."

Merkinder chose to ignore the implications in her statement, hearing his own teachings coming back to him. The child who carried the burden of Spirit always walked hand in hand with Melancholy and eventually made the acquaintance of Madness. The moment he awakened her with Knowledge, he doomed her with Awareness.

A faint drizzle had started to fall as it often did whenever he came out. He wondered if it waited for him. It dusted the shoulders of his very old suit, raising from the ashes of the past a scent of some cologne he had once worn. An unwelcome nostalgia stirred in him, a longing for something not only lost but obliterated. That he could not name it was irrelevant.

They walked in silence for a long time. Merkinder was content to listen to the rain as it plopped against the sea like a noisy splashing of mermaid tails. He had seen a mermaid once... somewhen back around the time the Crusaders were ransacking Constantinople, after his humanity had been sacrificed but before he had forgotten how it felt to *be* a man, to want the things men wanted. She was lounging on the shore on the outskirts of Pireaus when he came upon her. And to his surprise, she didn't dive back into the turquoise sea and he didn't try to drink her blood.

They were, in that moment, two transformed creatures looking at one another through a haze of mutual recognition and respect that transcended whatever labels they were carrying with them at the time. The main thing Merkinder remembered was that she had reached out to touch his wrist – her skin cold as the North Atlantic, fingers webbed like the feet of a sea bird. She said nothing, nor did he. It was enough simply to see one another, to know with certainty that there was at least one other who was not human, one other who knew the lonely embrace of immortality in a world where everything and everyone else were forever dying all around.

He did not remember what became of the mermaid, whether she went back to the sea, or if he simply walked on down the path in search of that something which had been torn from his soul when he lost his humanness in the embrace of a savage creator. All he remembered was that one single, wordless moment, when their eyes met and they both simply Knew... and it was enough.

"Was she beautiful?" Willow asked, drawing him out of his reverie.

The question took him off guard. "Was who beautiful?"

Willow actually laughed at him. "The woman – the one you were just thinking about," she replied as if he should have known. "You were light years in the past."

"A light year is a measurement of distance, not time," Merkinder said, though he knew he was hiding from the fact that Willow could clearly see right through him. It was not a sensation to which he was accustomed. Most of the children he had instructed over the infinite years were far too afraid of him to ever make personal connections – for he was, after all, a dark legend in the human world who might eat them up at any moment – and by the time they were old enough to figure out that he really was no danger to them, they had long since gone back to their own people. As they should. As they *must*.

His kind and their kind could not form lasting relationships. It would only end badly, and always the same. Humans were transient mortals. Not to be kept as lovers or pets. Fragile, ticking time bombs who would always turn to apple dust, fertilizer for the corn, food for the worms... dangerous playthings.

The air had turned colder, though Willow didn't seem to notice, even though her dress was rags held together by frayed threads. Her budding breasts pressed hard against the fabric which was too tight now to hold her as it had held her only a few months before.

Should he offer her his coat? Or would that simple gesture be misinterpreted?

He didn't like human conundrums, and was rusty in the social graces even though there were none left in the world. Impulsively, he took off the jacket, draping it around her narrow shoulders.

To his surprise, she snuggled into it, though the sleeves hung six inches below her fingertips and the shoulder seams sagged almost to her elbows. Flaring her nostrils, she sniffed at the lapel the way an animal might.

"I like it," she said. "Spicy musk and old cinnamon."

Merkinder was surprised that she could smell it at all. But then, Willow was the enigma.

Which made it all the harder for him to repeat, "You have to stop coming here, girl." He couldn't bring himself to say her name, afraid it might stick to his soul like honey. She didn't look up as they stood together at the edge of the sea, where timbers from a tall-masted sailboat protruded from the sand. Bones of the past. Skeletons in the graveyard of some other world, some other time. "Did you hear me?"

Her eyes were fixed on the horizon, on the burgundy apple which hung on the tree of temptation, but was really nothing more than the battered sun.

"I'm not going back," she said at last, her voice turning visible as it changed to mist and seemed to spell the letters out in the chilled air. What surprised Merkinder was the conviction with which she spoke, even if only at a whisper. "I'm staying with you – forever, I mean."

At this, Merkinder laughed – more in an attempt to take her off guard than out of any sense of amusement. "Stay? With *me*? Whatever *for*, girl?"

Lifting her eyes, she gave him a look such as one might give a stupid puppy. "We can grow pumpkins. We can be lovers." A pause, then: "You can make me like you." Another pause. "We both know you want to."

If Merkinder's heart had been beating, it probably would have stopped. He took a step back and looked at this blasphemous creature standing at the edge of a dead sea, draped in his coat like a hermit crab that had crawled inside the shell of some larger being. He didn't like the implications, for it wouldn't be much of a stretch to consider the possibility that she *had* gotten inside him.

"Where do you *get* such notions?" he asked, intentionally dismissive.

"From you, of course," she said with a lilt of amusement in her voice. "You shouldn't have taught me to read if you didn't want me to figure it out. You shouldn't have taught me to think if you didn't want me to see. I know what you are."

Merkinder's dark brows rose. "And what – *exactly* – do you think I am?"

Her soft laugh was siren song. "You taught me that love is the reason," she reminded him, and he couldn't deny the accusation even though it seemed to have very little to do with the question he had posed. "'Love is the equation', you always said. Well, if love is the equation, who are the integers if not ourselves?"

"You know nothing of love," Merkinder said abruptly, more harsh than he would have liked.

"I know enough," the girl-thing argued, though not with any sense of anger, instead a tone of lamentation and resignation. "If love is the catalyst of all creation, how can you manifest a new world if you're still creating the old world wrapped up in darkness? No one can serve two master – not even you. Can't have it both ways."

Spirit could be a pain in the ass. It posed as a girl-child, but spoke in a voice far beyond its years. Trickster and trouble-maker. Wisdom of winter incarnated as spring.

"It's not that simple," Merkinder stated, his voice barely audible over the gust that had come blowing in off the sea to listen. "The world is the world. Love is love."

"But everything begins with a thought," Willow reminded him. His own words. Haunting him again. Dangerous ghosts. "If we really *are* the creators of reality, then don't we have the responsibility to *do* something about it?"

"*Do* something?" Merkinder repeated, bordering on cruel, knowing what she was asking of him, knowing he couldn't – *wouldn't* – surrender to her desires. Desires she couldn't begin to understand, or so he told himself.

He took a step toward her, intentionally menacing, until they were only inches apart. Her human heat. His eternal cold. "What would you suggest, girl? Do you think it would make the world a better place if I tore away your clothes and ravaged your innocence, and took away the very things that make you *human*?"

For a single moment, he thought he saw fear in her eyes. But it was quickly replaced by the icy determination normally reserved for generals and executioners.

"Being human isn't all it's cracked up to be, Merkinder," she said, calling him by name for the first time in all the time he had known her. "You say you want the world to find its feet again, but I think you like things just the way they are. As long as the world wallows in death and darkness, you think you have some noble purpose to exist. But in the end, you're no different than the rest of us: just a lonely old man, lost and terrified."

Merkinder might have been offended had he been a man, had he been human. And maybe that made the point Willow seemed hell-bent on making. He hesitated. Looked away. Then quickly regrouped. Smiled in the way he had smiled when he was a hunter in search of human blood.

"I'm not like you," he reminded her, and reached out to brush the dark locks from her face. Seductive gesture. Distraction could hypnotize, mesmerize. It was legendary among his kind, after all. Leaning forward until he was only inches from her face, he whispered it again, lest there be any doubt. "I'm not like you, girl."

But Willow wasn't easily glamoured. Her eyes flashed, angry candles flickering in the wind. "If you could be human again – if you *could* be mortal again... *would* you?"

The seabird fell silent. The wind stopped. And that was the moment the student became the master.

"I'm going back to my house," Merkinder said sternly, ignoring the direct and dreadful question he had wrestled with for longer than he cared to remember. "You would be wise not to stay out when total darkness falls."

Willow said nothing, though he could feel her eyes on his retreating back.

"I'll be back tomorrow," she called after him. "And the day after that."

Turning, he looked at her through the cold veil Time had built around him. "Do as you *will*," he said, words often used with the children he had nurtured. They all knew what it meant: do what you have the free will and the force of intent to do. No easy task, even for an immortal.

Merkinder willed himself to walk back to the house and through the earthen walls without so much as another glance in the girl's direction. It was the most difficult thing he had done in the memory of Time.

***

Three years vanished. Merkinder did not know where they went, only that he awoke one evening to find them gone. Perhaps the pumpkins ate them. Perhaps the scarecrows chased them away. During that time, he did not go outside other than to feed, and that only twice. At his age, he did not need to drink blood anymore. Instead, he thrived on the perpetually self-renewing animus of Life, whether the essence of the humans or the jackrabbits who came to pilfer the garden, or simply from the Earth herself. That, too, was his nature – ironic when studied too closely. Merkinder the Wicked, king of the damned, now the custodian and guardian of Life – reverencing it more than any mortal ever had or ever could. Life... the pure urban poetry scrawled on the walls of the abyss.

That thought brought a sharp pain somewhere in the vicinity of his soul. He'd gotten used to playing the role of cold orb that ruled the night. And Willow had threatened to bring him back to life in a way he wasn't sure he wanted in the least. Who would turn whom? And into what?

Her question still hung in his ears, three years after the fact.

If you could be human again... would you?

"No being in their right mind would *choose* to be human!" he shouted into the cold, black air, acutely overwhelmed by the avalanche of feeling he had held in check for more centuries than even he could count. What sad, pitiful creatures they were – so lost out there in the darkness while Death stalked them and Pain nipped at their heels. So brave to keep going when all the odds and all the gods were stacked against them. So innocent that they could sing into the night that would eventually consume them and return them to the dust from which they came. How brave they were to love, secretly knowing that love would always end in grief.

A difficult breath grabbed his chest, caught in his throat, seized him by the shoulders and shook him until – eventually

– he realized he was sobbing, not for himself, but for every destitute, terrified, mystified mortal being who had ever lived, whether it walked on two legs or four, or slithered on its belly, or flew through the air on gossamer wings. They were all dying. Already dead. And that was simply that. In the end, it was nothing less than profane.

"My goodness!" Madness commented from darkness that smelled of still-born shadows and old snow. "You're carrying on as if this is some great revelation wrapped up for your birthday! Should I get you a tissue?"

Merkinder wept for three days and three nights, thoughts tumbling through his ravaged mind like evil acrobats.

And then, abruptly, something long forgotten emerged, buried so deep it must have crawled out the left nostril of some misshapen wormhole. The one and only thing his maker had told him on the night he himself gave up his humanity for a chance to live forever, on a night when he had begged for it and railed against it all in the same instant, when he had thrown himself at the feet of his maker, no longer certain if he were more afraid to die, or more afraid to go on living with the constant fear of Death itself.

That was what it meant to be human. Willow saw it. His maker had seen it.

To be human... To be driven mad, to live in a constant and gnawing state of fear which eventually consumed the soul and threw the mortal corpse out to rot. No streets paved with gold at the end of the leprechaun's rainbow. No castrati choirs of caroling angels heralding the birth of any god or goddess. Just the everlasting, unending, tormenting darkness from which the first suffering soul must certainly have sprung at a time before Time got his name and became The Almighty Dick.

He didn't remember much about the transformation itself. Only that it was brutal. Without tenderness. Without kindness.

The screaming as his body was torn away from his soul. The pain like nothing he could have imagined. The journey through death and unimaginable hell and then the climb. The creation of the self from the nothing. The raising of the dead from the mire of slaughtered souls. The gathering of an identity where none had existed before. Spontaneous parthenogenesis. And then... simply...

I-Am.

"'Love is not kind or gentle. Love is evolution,'" his maker said, just before he left the room, never to be seen again. "'One day, if the fates are kind, you will remember that and act upon it.'"

Merkinder stopped breathing. *Love is evolution.*

"Disappointed?" Madness asked, drawing him back into whatever reality passed for the Now. "Would it be easier if Love were flowers and heart-shaped chocolates and Hallmark sentiments on old parchment? Gag me... where's my insulin?"

Ignoring the voice of Madness, Merkinder rolled slowly from the bed which was once a plush mattress, but which now more resembled a pile of rags scattered with leaves that had found their way in through some crack in the everything. The living room remained dark, with only a faint red sunglow from the window facing the sea.

He should have been surprised to see Willow sitting on the shore, her back to his house, but somehow, he wasn't surprised in the least.

Unoffended by being shunned, Madness sidled up next to him, whispering close to his ear. "Did you think you could dangle love and eternity in front of them forever and not have one of them eventually tell you to put up or shut up?"

The comment was far too lucid, considering the source.

To escape it, Merkinder flowed through the wall to find himself on the beach – though in hindsight, he had no real recollection of willing the action. It just seemed the right thing to do, leading to where he wanted to be, even if he had no idea what he intended to do.

Willow looked up, sensing his approach, and as he moved to sit down next to her on the cinder-shore, he realized she was still wearing the jacket he had given her more than three years in the past. Her fingertips had found their way to the ends of the sleeves, the shoulders no longer as all-consuming as they had been the day he had first draped it around her.

She had grown her bones, filled out her skin.

"I wasn't sure you'd come," she said, leaning against him as if he were her rightful place.

"I wasn't sure I would either," Merkinder confessed. The warm weight of her was distracting, comforting. A duality. He didn't move away even though Madness had come out to watch, and was reciting a long list of the sins and the dangers Merkinder was courting.

"What was the sunrise like?" she asked, taking him momentarily off guard, picking up the conversation where it had left off a very long time ago, when she was still a student and he was her mentor.

"My kind doesn't exactly court the dawn," he reminded her, mildly amused. "But from what I remember, it was warm, golden."

"Like honey dripped over the earth by faeries," Willow commented, her voice distant, contemplative.

"Yes... I suppose. Something like that."

Cocking her dark head, she studied him. "Does it hurt you? The light, I mean."

Empathy and compassion. Concern for another. He had seen no indication of it in the humans until that moment. Almost without volition, he put an arm around her back, filled with affection which was largely unwanted, but entirely overwhelming. "No," he said at last. "The light no longer hurts me."

The girl sighed, relieved. A seabird piped. Further away, another answered. From the edge of the forest, a pale dog watched – not with hunger, but curiosity. Small waves lapped at the shore, murmuring secrets.

Merkinder thought of the mermaid, wondered if she were flapping her tail on the bottom of the ocean, causing the sea to rock, wondering if she had gone deep to wait, just as he himself had waited.

From high up in the forest, a baby cried. A woman's voice barked a command. A man was singing.

"The world is coming back to life," Merkinder whispered, not realizing he had spoken aloud. The thought was exhilarating, disturbing. The thought was terrifying.

"She'll need a mother and a father," Willow said, never one for being subtle. "At least until the pumpkins know which way to grow and the humans find their Dreaming again."

Merkinder wasn't at all sure he was qualified to father a world. But who was? "And then?"

Pressed tight against him, Willow shrugged. "Then we'll get fat and lazy and grow old together in rocking chairs on the porch."

Merkinder laughed, mildly surprised that he still could, for what was looming before him was daunting. Where she had learned the lore of rocking chairs and couples growing old together, he did not know. Perhaps, he conceded, it was simply universal., and so he made a mental note to include Woodworking in his teachings.

"You do realize I've never done this before," he cautioned her, knowing full well that she knew full well what he was talking about. "What if it doesn't work?"

Stretching upward, her lips pressed to his ear, the voice of Spirit asked, "What if it *does*?"

She had a point. He had been old too long. Dead too long.

Time to stop holding the world in darkness. Time to absorb the lessons he had taught the children for centuries. *Everything begins with a thought. Reality is entirely self-created. You have to be immortal before you can know how to become immortal. The destruction of faith is the beginning of evolution. To allow the impossible is to do the impossible. Love is the reason and the equation.*

Willow had been brought to him as a sacrifice.

She tasted of pine and promise, cool green moss and morning dew. Silk chalice, opened to shatter the spell, to release the night and summon the dawn. He sank deep, drank deep.

Love is evolution.

***

About the Author...

Della Van Hise is a native of Florida, transplanted to California at the age of 21, who has subsequently sunk her roots into the high desert near Joshua Tree National Park. She has not personally seen any aliens since around 1992, but there is rumored to be a secret UFO base underneath her house.

Della's writing started around age 11 on an old Smith Corona typewriter. No, not an electric one. A real antique, made of metal and heavier than a wet coffin. Her first professional novel was best-selling KILLING TIME - the controversial Star Trek novel which was recalled and re-edited in 1984 (making the first edition a rare collector's item) - and which was the foundational plot for the STAR TREK "Reboot" movie.

Della has written extensively in the non-fiction genre, with titles such as QUANTUM SHAMAN: DIARY OF A NAGUAL WOMAN and SCRAWLS ON THE WALLS OF THE SOUL. "Quantum Shaman" focuses heavily on the author's metaphysical explorations and experiences, while "Scrawls" is a continuation of those journeys many years later. If you enjoyed the works of Carlos Castaneda or Don Miguel Ruiz, you'll enjoy the non-fiction works of Della Van Hise.

Della shares her life with her significant other, Wendy Rathbone, and a variety of cats, dogs and desert wildlife.

———

If you enjoyed Dangerous Playthings, please consider these other exemplary works by the same author...

The Effect of Moonlight on Tombstones
(A Dark Little Collection of Poetry Gleaned from the Gnosis of Vampyres and Songs of the Muse)
Della Van Hise

———

Candles keep journals
of time's passing
in empty books of matches.

———

My heart is a haunted room,
sinister sanctuary.
When it breaks,
shattered by your sharp white smile,
all the shadows come leaking out,
phantoms of neverland
loosed on the world of men.

On Amazon or directly from the publisher at
www.eyescrypublications.com

NO FORWARDING ADDRESS
Della Van Hise

When Terrans came to sail dark seas,
And see what stars might be...
Heaven moved with no forwarding address,
And left this void to me.
(Children's song from Lazali)

———————

A literary science fiction novel told in the voice of an empath, *No Forwarding Address* explores the lures and the dangers of love, the tragedies and triumphs stirring in the human heart.

When Crystal and Raine first meet, it is 50 years after The Great War on Earth. They are hesitant to trust, afraid to love. But even if they are able to overcome these seemingly insurmountable obstacles, is even love enough?

When a man has the stars in his eyes, legend says he must serve them above all others.

———————

I knew then that it wasn't love and hate who were mirror twins. The final irony was that grief *would always turn out to be the paradoxical antithesis and simultaneous manifestation of whatever it is that humans call love.*

Crystal remained silent and walked a few steps away from Raine – further down the shoreline, until she stood under the wing of one fallen Phantom. She thought of the ship she had seen from the balcony of our home, and though it had long since disappeared over the dark and treacherous abyss of the ocean, its image lingered clearly in her thoughts. On that ship was a man, she thought. A terribly lonely man who made no great difference to the flow of time or the memory of the galaxy. A man who, like Raine, was compelled to keep moving and look only ahead and never behind. A man who could not afford the luxury of waving goodbye to friends on shore.

At last, she turned toward her beloved and watched him watching the darkness. He stood only a few feet away, yet the images in my mind said he might as well have been a million light years off in the void. He was lost to her in that instant out-of-time, just as lost and impossible to find as the light from that ship which had vanished over the horizon..

Available on Amazon or from the publisher at.
www.eyescrypublications.com

COYOTE
Della Van Hise

A Novel of Love, Honor and Personal Sacrifice...

When River Willows is accused of a murder she didn't commit, her life takes a turn toward the sanctuary of a world existing at right-angles to our own. Combining the mysticism of martial arts and the romantic conflict of a young woman torn between two powerful men, COYOTE takes the reader on an epic journey of dangerous secrets, military cover-ups, and the infinite heart of the peaceful warrior.

"So who's Coyote?" I asked, trying to ignore the effect he was having on me. "You?"

Steale laughed easily, though it did little to hide the torment behind that mask of indifference he wore so well.

"Coyote's a scavenger, Jack of all trades. The Native Americans call him the trickster - the one who brought chaos down on the world." He shrugged as if altogether unconcerned. "Original sin."

"Is that what you are?" I asked, keeping it light despite the growing knot my stomach. "Original sin?"

He kept his profile to me, eyes straight ahead as he drove. "Sure you want to know?"

I couldn't help wondering if I had cornered the coyote, or if the clever trickster had cornered me.

By the author of **KILLING TIME** – without a doubt the most controversial **STAR TREK** novel ever published!

From the author:
www.eyescrypublications.com

On Amazon
http://www.amazon.com/Coyote-Della-Van-Hise/dp/0976689782/

Also Available From Eye Scry Publications...

Thorn may be an 800 year old vampire, but he does not possess the ability to create others of his kind, and so he is cursed to fall in love with mortals, only to watch them grow old and die.

Torn by grief, Thorn denounces his immortality and enters into a comatose oblivion for decades. When he awakens, he is no longer in London, but finds himself in a world spun into being by his own desires - a world where Time and Death do not exist, a world where it is forever autumn, where the Parish of Shadows and the River of Stars become his home.

It is in this world of Umberlight that he meets Atom - an interloper into his private sanctuary, but also an impudent imp who is destined to reveal to Thorn the three dangerous elements a vampire must possess in order to become a Creator.

The Art of Brutality.
Submission to Dark Desire.
Love.

_____

One reader said: "This is erotica at its best!" We think you'll agree.
Written in a poetic and literary voice by a respected professional author.

TALES OF UMBERLIGHT promises to be an exciting new series for fans of vampire erotica, paranormal romance and just plain good story-telling. *Prince of Umberlight* is the first book in a series. Story lines have been outlined for the next two books, with Book 2 scheduled to be completed in the fall/winter of 2015.

On Amazon or from www.eyescrypublications.com

YEAR OF THE RAM
Della Van Hise

Year of the Ram was described by one reviewer as... "A space-faring gay romance full of love, angst, and longing."

Only after Star Commander Morgan Diego becomes an exile as a result of a Galaxy Corps political blunder does he begin to realize how much he valued the companionship of his second in command - the mysterious Lucien, an Alfarian who is more elven than human, with peculiar powers & abilities which begin to unfold as he, too, realizes what he has lost.

Separated by circumstance from his former life, Morgan is thrust into a world where he must survive by his wits. When he meets a peculiar little old man calling himself Kim Le, Morgan finds himself in a situation where he is required to master The Art - not only a form of human & extraterrestrial martial arts, but a way of living and being that will alter his life forever.

At the temple, he is introduced to his new teacher, another Alfarian who begins to steal his heart - a heart which is already promised to Lucien. Torn and conflicted, Morgan struggles with the world he left behind and the world he now inhabits.

Beginning to believe he may never again return to his ship and to the friends and loved ones he left behind, he is all the more frustrated and heartbroken when a new Master arrives at the temple: a man to whom Morgan is immediately drawn both mentally and physically, a man who is strikingly familiar... yet utterly alien.

Year of the Ram is a fully-fleshed novel, approximately 97000 words, with a focus on the love story and romance angle. Set against a science fiction milieu, it explores the infinite possibilities of the human and alien heart. Sexual content is explicit, though is not the primary focus of the novel.

For those who like a romance that forces its characters to contemplate the ecstasies AND the agonies of love... you will enjoy *Year of the Ram* immensely.

On Amazon or directly from the publisher at
www.eyescrypublications.com

LETTERS TO AN ANDROID

Wendy Rathbone

Cobalt is a created human, vat grown and born adult, with no human rights and indentured to serve others for the duration of his life. Liyan is a young man with wanderlust in his eyes, embarking on a career that takes him to the furthest regions of space. The two become unlikely friends and create a memorable long-distance correspondence. Through Liyan, Cobalt gets to explore the universe, living vicariously through his friend's wave transmissions. A strong bond develops between them that not even the stars can put asunder.

Now you know an android who writes poetry.

This is all your fault. Did you not read my last wave telling you extracurricular activities for my kind are discouraged? Of course this is harmless and strangely enjoyable and does not necessarily require me to leave the hotel. Pel would not care if I wrote lines of equations or nonsensical juxtaposed words. As long as the act does not bring my mental state into question.

However, in history, poetry is often written by the rebels.

So we can keep this to ourselves.

Let me know about your lieutenant's test.

And to give you peace of mind, I never believed you observed me as anything other than human.

Some people are and always will be hateful bigots. Most people are simply uncomfortable in speaking to "property." And anyway, friendship, like poetry, is also discouraged.

Your friend,
Cobalt

www.eyescrypublications.com
Also on Amazon

PALE ZENITH
Wendy Rathbone
A Science Fiction Novel

On a far-flung "Earth" in a parallel universe, two factions are fighting a decades-long psychic war. Young talented psychics are being temporarily kidnapped from present day Earth, seemingly at random, to serve as part of one side's psychic army. They are put under the control of spychiatrists, mysterious machines with many limbs that have a programmed ability to travel time and space and universes to kidnap and control carefully selected humans. The humans never know they are being used; when their missions are completed they are brought back to their universe through time and placed back in their beds, their memories wiped.

_____

The shadows wound the tall corridor in muted gold, varnished brown. It seemed as though they were in the bowels of a giant serpent coiled outside time, outside space.

When they left the palace, a familiar sun flourished in a clear, blue sky. But this wasn't their sun. Not Zack's sun. It was an alien star burning within a different galaxy in an all too distant universe. Zack looked up squinting, trying to see if he could peer beyond the sky, beyond the pale of midday and into his own timespace, but there was nothing. Only sunlight. Only the thin atmosphere of an Earth not his own.

His back knotted again. Leo's presence was a gelid space inside his chest, empty. Always before he'd felt a warmth there, a sort of pressure like someone's hand pressed gently to his heart. He'd taken Leo for granted knowing, the way a shadow falls when you block the sun, that he was there around him, inside him: blood, air, salt, brain, soul. They were genetic duplicates, twins, spiritual halves. Without him, Zack knew the first icy tugs of panic.

FROM THE AUTHOR
www.eyescrypublications.com
ON AMAZON
http://www.amazon.com/Pale-Zenith-Wendy-Rathbone/dp/0976689790/

Eye Scry Publications
A Visionary Publishing Company
www.eyescrypublications.com